y	Ch
th	Sh
ch	Y
sh	X
x	Th

“Good morning, Sheep!” yells Fox Cub.

"Thanks, Chicken!" Fox Cub yells.

Next morning, Fox Cub feels unwell.

His throat is sore.

Fox Cub has a rash, too.

Doctor Yak tells Fox Cub's mom that Fox Cub must rest his throat.

"Rest is boring!" thinks Fox Cub.

Fox Cub's mom brings him a hot lemon drink.

"It throbs," yelps Fox Cub.

Hush, Fox Cub.
Sleep.

Sh!
Zzzzzz